Table of Conte

Foreword - by Frederick Quin Esq.

Chapter 1 - Greetings

Chapter 2 - Starting the show: "Anyone in from overseas? Report them to the authorities."

Chapter 3 - The Rules: schooling these retards

Chapter 4 - Getting the audience onside: suck up like a champ

Chapter 5 - Cheerleaders: how to spot them

Chapter 6 - Splitting the audience into teams: the ABC of singling out a troublesome fuckwit

Chapter 7: Gittin dem lolz: don't be too funny, the acts are shit

Chapter 8: Racial slurs: when to use them

Chapter 9: Introducing a woman: how to lower expectations

Chapter 10: But what if I'm a woman: when nature hates you

Chapter 11: Calling an interval: do it like a boss

Chapter 12: Chatting to the audience during an interval: getting that dick wet

Chapter 13: Closing the show: "I'm on Twitter…"

Further reading

Index

FOREWORD by Frederick Quin Esq.

Dave ask right forward his book on comparing I said yes cos he directed my first our long show and did good

Wen I rote my book on comparing I took Davez know ledge and made it my own

This wrong and I shud of asked him b4 I did this Dave better then me u should by his book he knew what he's talking about

When 1st started comedy I looked Dave and new one day I wud be bringing him to stage   Dave is 1 of best and you can lern him if you follow destructions

I love comedy and look at it a lot I have to say that dave looks best

I did jokes about trannies and got in bovver cos I dint listen Dave now I wish I had   Red Redmond got angry becos that is what he does now I proper regret some things I was court doing People like jokes sometimes they like jokes that bad but that does not meen I shud do those jokes even if funny

I MC a lot when they carnt get some1 else I am better cos I have red this book   This book is proper and will make you best wish had not wrote my book now this cheaper

I wud like to thank Dave for his advises over years and his encooridgement growing my beard   The beard ment I don't need a person ality the crowd like how friendly I look so it helped me MC love and energy

I reco mend this book   It will make you top MC wever not you want to you could be

I have a cute dog WOOF WOOF WOOF

Chapter 1 - Greetings!

Thank you for purchasing this book. Within these pages is everything you need to know to take you from the level of a Spiky Mike, all the way up to to a Stephen Grant. At each stage, we will address how the glue of all comedy nights can be refined into a Pritt Stick of genius that will leave most audience members asking why you don't give stand up comedy a try, as you are just as funny as the acts.

Compering is a tricky beast to master. Some will say that you need years of experience to get good at it, others will tell you it's what poor stand up comedians with no discernible personality do to help keep their diary full. Regardless, this book will help you to become the compere you always knew you could be. I'll take you from a beginner, to someone who can compere a big weekend comedy club like a professional even though you still have to work a day job. WE WILL ALSO COVER ADVANCED TECHNIQUES (WHATEVER THE FUCK THEY ARE)

We'll cover everything a compere needs to know, as well as telling you a lot of stuff you probably don't need to know. So, let's crack on shall we?

GIVE ME A CHEER IF YOU ARE READY FOR THE FIRST CHAPTER?

Chapter 2 - Starting the show: "Anyone in from overseas? Report them to the authorities…"

This is critical to the beginning of the evening. If you don't start the show, nobody will know what to do, and the audience will just sit there waiting to be entertained and, if not given direction, they'll starve to death. A professional gig will have introductory music, an off stage mic and perhaps even a professional who gives a countdown to the beginning of a show. But what if it's a Mirth Control gig? Well, this is where the compere dons his cape and becomes the hero that Exeter deserves.

The compere should cup his hands around his mouth in order to better amplify his voice and announce to the audience that show will start in five minutes time. Then (if you have the confidence) a direction to the audience to perhaps empty their bladders or get a drink as once the show has started, it will be impossible for them to do this, as the law states that once a show has started, you have to remain seated and with whatever hydration you had at the time the gig started.

Sometimes, you might have to announce yourself on to stage. Now, this might break the illusion of showbiz, but don't be put off by such an occurrence. Many of the all time greats of compering have had to do this, and you shouldn't feel like a loser just because the 5 people who've turned up to the pub gig you've arranged because you're trying to impress Tina, are annoyed that the TV has been turned off. Fuck those guys: you need to talk at them awkwardly for fifteen minutes before getting your open spot mate on.

And Tina rang in sick.

PRO TIP: Don't shout "Show starts in five minutes you smelly fucking cunts"

Once you climb the ladder of comedy, starting the show becomes much easier. You should concentrate on how you walk onto the stage, and how much of an alpha male you seem. It is very important that the audience trusts you to shepherd them through the show they've paid £15 to watch, so you must go on and assert your dominance. Do this by fucking one of the females on the front row, preferably one with a man that she is married to. Maintain full eye contact with the audience, and just before climax, withdraw your penis and ejaculate all over two or three of the males on the front row. Dominance shown, you will now be able to begin the show like a boss.

One of the things that I believe Steve Bennett looks for in his comperes is lots of hot sticky loads fired straight at his face. All of his favourite comperes have probably ejaculated onto his bespectacled face - many of them all at the same time. One of the main reasons that his spelling is so bad is because of the all the crusty spunk that is in his eyes. If you want a good review for your compering (and as a result of the good reviews, the respect of the entire industry) you have to make sure that you have a couple of loads ready to go on any particular night, just in case he's in. Sometimes he'll want it in his mouth but pay no heed to his demands: straight on his mush.

Once all this is done, you need to take the microphone out of the stand and speak in to it. A funny accent is a great way to break the ice, with the funniest being Chinese or Bangladeshi. Although cliched, saying hello and welcoming the audience to the show is a solid way to start the gig. It might seem simple, but I cannot count the number of times that comperes have gone on and shouted "Heil Hitler!" at an audience and immediately made it more difficult for themselves.

Ideally, you want to start friendly so that they can quickly forget about the showing of dominance.

If it is a new gig, it is important to reference that at the top and get your excuses in early for why you are a deeply unfunny cunt who shouldn't be allowed anywhere near a stage. Have your life crisis elsewhere eh? The audience will need to know what's what and how and audience should behave. But just because it's a new gig, it doesn't mean that long running gigs don't need the audience telling how to behave. They've paid their money, so it's up to you to tell them how to use that opportunity.

Chapter 3 - The Rules: schooling these retards

Part of the compere's job is to let the audience know what is and isn't acceptable behaviour at a comedy show. Lots of comperes neglect to mention the rules at the top of a show and this means that the bouncers might end up actually having to do some fucking work instead of watching comedy for free every night.

The key with laying down the law is to do it in a friendly fashion, with a little twinkle in the eye and tug on the dick. Don't bellow "NO TALKING WHILST THE ACTS ARE ON STAGE!" as this will just make the audience despise you for reminding them of a school teacher. Instead, hand each of them a leaflet with how they should behave, and have them read it at their own pace whilst you provide incidental music on a harp.

PRO TIP: avoid wearing blackface

"But," I hear you ask, like the pathetic newbie and/or shit act with years under your belt, "what are the rules?" Well, thank god I'm here to tell you the rules. Be sure to lay them out in detail just after the beginning of each show, and make sure that you say them with authority.

Rule 1: No talking when the acts are on stage

Rule 2: Put your mobile phones on to silent, unless you've got a baby sitter, but there's not much you can do when you're at the gig so just let the baby die FFS

Rule 3: Before laughing at any racially charged humour, look to see if there are any in the room and gauge whether or not you should laugh based on their reaction

Rule 4: Respect people's personal space (I'm looking at you Ahmed)

Rule 5: If you want to chat to anyone, chat to me because I don't have good enough material to be an act

Rule 6: Laugh at my shitty joke about pagers

Rule 7: Just relax and have fun, even though I've just saddled you with a load of rules you probably already knew because most of you are decent human beings but if I don't do it I am somehow responsible if the first act has a shit gig

Society needs rules, and the comedy club is no different. You are the new Mayor of Mongtown and these pitiful people who help to pay your wages need indoctrinating to your way of thinking, so that the professional comedians can have an easier time of it. If the comedy club was to actually have rules with any sense of justice, we'd be able to walk on with a shotgun and just make society better by eliminating the rudest cunts ever to walk the face of the earth. And we'd also have a rule about the audience not applauding like Pavlovian dogs whenever a guitar act finishes their shitty song and strums their 6 string cheat machine in a pleasing manner. That SHOULD be rule number one, giving the audience some power and ability to administer justice. But no, we tell them that they shouldn't talk.

We tell them that it's rude and that it's bad for the atmosphere, which to a certain extent is true in professional comedy clubs. But if some poor fucker is sitting through 10 open spots in a pub and each act only has 2 minutes of decent material with the rest of it being just poorly thought out shite, don't think you're doing the world a favour by telling the audience they can't talk through that shower of suicide inducing dog shit. Lives have been saved as a result of audience members taking it upon themselves to limit their misery by quietly distracting themselves via the medium of conversation, as the 55 year old menopausal woman bleats on stage about her sons growing up and leaving her at home alone.

I mean, fucking hell. Some of the shite I've had to sit through, it's a wonder the audience didn't riot, never mind have a little chat amongst themselves.

Anyway, cover your arse and tell them not to chat, that way you can't be held responsible. FFS, what a terrible state of affairs. Oh, here's a good one: if there's a married couple in, reference that they've come on a night out where they can't talk to one another and how shit their marriage must be. It's tried and tested and it'll make everyone laugh at the fleeting nature of love, distracting them momentarily from the the fact that they too are pursuing such relationship goals, so that they may continue to run from the existential crisis that grips us all as we fumble our way through this thing called life.

Chapter 4 - Getting the audience onside: suck up like a champ

So, you've started the show and you've got the rules established, but the audience still hates you. What to do? Assuming you are a straight white male (and why wouldn't you be?) you will have none of the other excuses to fall back on that those left leaning snowflake weaklings do. You're gonna have to knuckle down and get the audience onside.

Getting the audience onside can be a tricky affair, and will depend greatly upon where you are gigging and who you are gigging to. If you're compering in a professional comedy club, it will be easy to get them onside by talking about how Thatcher was a cunt and Trump is a nasty piece if work. You should also reference what a terrible thing racism is, and that you are a feminist. Don't worry about providing evidence for your claim of being a feminist, if you say it with enough sincerity those thick cunts will lap it up anyway. Indeed, many of the most disgusting sex perverts in comedy have claimed to be feminists, so don't let that stop you from spinning out more of your own horse shit.

But what if you're dealing with a more intelligent audience? People who sometimes listen to Radio 4 and pass it off as their own opinion? Well, for this you're gonna have to use some of those tried and tested stock phrases. These phrases are useful because they contain code words that help an audience to relax and trust you. I'm going to give you both the phrases and the translation, so that you can better tune in to your audience and be a more effective compere.

PHRASE	TRANSLATION
'What a lovely part of the world…'	'You have no immigration here'
'What a lovely audience!'	'You're even laughing at my shit jokes'
'Let's see who we've got in tonight…'	'Just checking for wheelchairs and carers…'
'I've worked with all these acts…'	'Trust me, it gets better'
'Who's been to live comedy before?'	'Fucking Jesus Christ you cunts are thick'
'I gig all over the country'	'I can't get weekends'
'I'm here to steer the ship'	'I wish I was in the navy for the bumming'
'Consider me your fluffer…'	'I am a deeply unoriginal thinker'
'The more love and support you show…'	'This next act is a right needy fucker'
'You lot are bloody lovely!'	'PLEASE LIKE ME! I AM SHIT!"

Getting the audience onside can be an arduous task, especially when you don't have any of the material, charisma or improvisational skills necessary to be a good compere. But plenty of hobbyists are still clogging up the circuit and clinging on to a dream that will never happen, so why should it stop you?

PRO TIP: Don't rape your colleagues

There's an old showbiz trick that works a treat when an audience is as impenetrable as a #metoo comedienne, and that is to use reverse psychology on them. Tell them you don't even want them to like you, and they'll like you all the more. Try and be as obnoxious a cunt as possible and watch them fall into your arms like a jilted lover being allowed back for one more anal experiment, before you realise it's just not for you.

You have to remind the audience that this is a two way street, and that the reason they might not be enjoying themselves has nothing to do with the quality of the acts that they are enduring. No, no, no. It's THEM. They need to get on board and stop being so difficult to please in order for them to have a good night. It's your job as a compere to remind them of this.

'But what if I've tried everything and they still won't get onside?'

Jesus. You really are shit aren't you? At times like this you'll need to go around and perform oral sex on each audience member, not stopping until you've made each person climax in your mouth. Everyone has a different technique but you'll have to adapt to the situation depending on the age of the audience. As with everything comedy related, kids shows are the hardest when it comes to using this technique. Make sure that you have each child's permission before beginning your journey in the Land of no Pubes, and be prepared to met by an awkward silence as you perform.

Chapter 5 - Cheerleaders: how to spot them

Using a member of the audience to start a round of applause can be a very effective way of bringing the room around to focus on one person, as you magnanimously defer some of your responsibility on to a paying customer. You want someone not too shy, but not a complete show steeling fuckwit. You also don't want anybody conspicuous for reasons to do with God punishing them for past life sins and genetics.

What we want to achieve by using a cheerleader is for these fucking idiot monkeys to focus on a fellow pleb, just before they start clapping for the anonymous person whose name they've just been informed of - but have already forgotten. The cheerleader is the bridge between the talent and the great unwashed, but you must be careful in your selection process as this cheerleader could end up steeling the show.

The ideal cheerleader will be 18-25 years old, curvy but with long legs, sexually adventurous but not too experienced, with stunning dark hair and a sexy, husky laugh. She'll want to do your bidding both on and off the stage, with each interaction with her only serving to increase the sexual tension between each of you. Sure, you're over 40 years old, but her Dad didn't get that car he'd promised to on her 17th birthday, and now she wants to pay him back by passionately fucking someone exactly the same age.

PRO TIP: wear two condoms

Laura won't leave you alone for the next few years, randomly turning up to gigs she doesn't even live near just to freak you the fuck out. Don't believe any of the photos she sends you about her being pregnant either, as they can easily be photoshopped nowadays and it isn't even necessarily *her* pregnancy test. Sure, the baby LOOKS like you but lots of babies have generic features that they'll grow out of. The key thing is to not put anything incriminating on a message that can have screen shot taken of. Use the Signal app on a separate phone that you only switch on when you want to get your dick wet or send/receive a photo.

Your wife will want to know what's going on and why you seem so stressed, but you should've spent years convincing her by now that any suspicions she's got about your infidelity are delusions on her part and that she's probably going mad.

Changing your name to a stage name can really help in this situation, in fact changing your name every single gig will help make things more difficult for you when Laura starts getting the fucking CSA involved. How can it be legal for them to compel you to prove you're not the father? I mean, what kind of country is it, where a woman can just lie down and get herself filled up with all sorts of random jizz, then expect men to pick up the tab when her benefits get stopped?

Why did she even leave home? I get that you have to tell the council that you're homeless and with a child in order to secure a decent house, but there are limits to my patience and I'm sorry, I want nothing to do with little Jamie.

It's also important that your cheerleader knows what is expected of them. Patronise them by doing a little practise first, so that they don't fuck it up. I like to do things on a count of three so that things are kept simple. I like a simple life, and I'll be damned if I'm paying for two families when all I was after was the ego boost of knowing that I can still pull a sexy bird if I put my mind to it.

How was I supposed to know she was a psycho? Fucking 3am she turned up at my house demanding to give me a blow job. Demanding! She nearly woke up my wife and I had to go down and let her suck me off at the side of the house. She threatened to tell everyone what I was doing and I almost had a nervous breakdown trying to keep it all secret. And for what? Now everyone knows, and I'm back to where I was when I started comedy: living in a house with three other socially retarded open spots who couldn't write a joke if their lives depended on it.

Chapter 6 - Splitting the audience into teams: the ABC of singling out a troublesome fuckwit

Another classic tactic of getting the audience to applaud properly is to split the audience in to teams. You're not actually splitting them into teams (lol) at all. No, what you're actually doing is ostracising a member of the audience that you have deemed to be trouble in that annoyingly attention seeking way that could probably derail the gig.

This cunt has piped up one too many times and you don't have the skill to shut him up, nor enough trust in the staff to get this idiot removed. This fucking moron will continue to pose problems throughout the night, and is playing up both to the group that allows him to be a member, as well as the audience. This prick is getting laughs that should be yours, and has twice the charisma you do, so this will require careful handling to make it look like you are in control of the situation. This is where the method of splitting the audience in to teams comes in to play.

You split the audience down the middle, with one side being Team A, the other side being Team B. However (and this is where it gets really cunning) you have a trick up your sleeve for that cunt everyone has pretty much forgotten about. You mention Team C.

"But wait! The room has been evenly split! There can't possibly be another team! What does this comedic genius have in store for us?!"

Team C is the prick. Trust me, this will take your PMSL to a ROFL. By making this individual Team C, you give the unbelievable twat a chance to get it all out their system.

PRO TIP: don't split the room by colour of skin

You ask Team A to show you what they've got, then you ask Team B, then you ask Team C. This is where the attention seeking retard can really go at it, but it also has the impact of killing a little bit of their soul, as the power has now been reversed and they are doing your bidding. Even if they don't play along, it's because a bit of them deep inside knows that they are an awful shitbag of misery. You give them just enough attention to satiate their hunger for love, but also just enough to help them become self aware. Your goal here is to make the night run more smoothly, and facilitate the eventual suicide of Team C.

Another way of splitting the audience in to teams with a view to eventually bring them together is to split the via gender.

Now, the terms Gender and Sex have kind of become interchangeable, but that is largely due to the increasing popularity of Gender Studies in academia, which was created in the main by Simone de Beauvoir and is largely to do with a refusal to accept biological facts and has more to do with a philosophy that stipulates that social conditioning is responsible for gender rather than biology. This is all part of a creeping radical left ideology that will help sweep in a new and more extreme form of socialism which will then lead on to a crushing totalitarian state of communism where comedy will no longer be allowed.

As such, try not to refer to any of this and simply ask the audience to cheer if they're a woman, and then cheer if they're a man. This will help them be able to self identify as whichever gender they choose, and will keep you out of trouble. There may be an androgynous looking thing with blue hair and obvious breasts that feels left out, but that's tough shit. Maybe use the disabled toilet if you don't want to be labeled as a man or a woman?

Once the women have cheered as women, have the women then cheer like men (keep an eye on the blue haired dungarees wearer, see what xe does) and then do the same for men, but in reverse. Rejoice in the high pitched squeals as men try to sound like women, and women go deeper to sound like men. Then appreciate that high and low pitch voices that each gender has is to do with the biology of hormones and how the body changes during puberty: not which toys you played with as a child.

Some of this might sound controversial. There are two ways to deal with this: one is to announce early on in the gig that you are a feminist and wait for the applause. The other is to say that you do a lot of gigs for the troops.

Chapter 7: Gittin dem lolz: don't be too funny, the acts are shit

One of the biggest problems facing a compere is being much, much funnier than any of the acts on the bill. With the exception of Spiky Mike, this will happen at some point in your career and must be dealt with in a sympathetic manner.

Basically, fuck the other acts. These cunts need to up their game if they're gonna survive in this industry. We are all on stage fighting for our lives, and you need to use every tool at your disposal in order to git dem lolz and make sure your diary is full. If you know the acts on the bill, make sure you do their bankers before bringing them on.

Some comedians think that a comedy night is a team event. HELL NO! We comedians are Thatcherite wet dreams of gushing squirt, and each of us needs to keep the other on their toes by deliberately sabotaging one another. Solidarity is for communists and last I checked, we lived in Great Britain. Jeremy Corbyn will never seize power, no matter how attractive his anti-semitic polices are.

Don't be shy about taking a guitar on stage to compere with either. Encore that fucker if you need to, show those fuckers who is the boss. Get the audience doing some kind of chant as you bring the first act to the stage, whatever it takes. A rising tide raises all ships, but you want a tsunami of compering to drown those cunts. Over run, drain the audience of any attention span and then get that fucking cunt on stage.

PRO TIP: crush your enemies, see them driven before you, and hear the lamentation of their women!

New Year's Eve many years ago, John Ryan did 45 minutes instead of a 20 minute set, getting the audience on stage and having them all stand and sing. It was a monumental display of cuntery from an opening act, and one that I have never forgotten. Here, the compere's job was to reset the room and make the gig as playable for the next act as possible. On that night, the next act was me. The compere ran on stage and said "John Ryan everyone! Keep that applause going and welcome your next act… Dave."

Absolutely top notch compering. I could see why he was a Jongleurs regular, and why that club closing down was a tragedy for the industry and every lazy hack cunt that ever worked for them. The compere that night really forced me to raise my game, as I gently shepherded the audience back to their seats and showed them where the toilet was. I gladly informed the audience that the bar was indeed open and they were serving drinks.

There are levels to this shit, and this was compering of the highest calibre. In order to keep the show to time, this cunt threw me under the bus and made me look like a shit comic who couldn't follow a guitar act with no discernible jokes. I have never gotten rid of that shame, and although typing this has been cathartic, I am still driven by a sense of revenge that I hope never leaves me.

One day, when my career is on a downward trajectory, I will share a bill with John Ryan. Maybe I'll be some poor labourer who has to endure a mental health training course run by John, or maybe I'll be in a room above a pub at an open mic night. But mark my words, John Ryan will pay for what he did to me that night. During circle time when we're passing around the emotion cushion, Bill the plasterer will hand it to me, and very ounce of hatred I've had festering in me since that night will come pouring out. I will scream in his face that a song with the chorus "We all just want to get drunk" isn't in any way shape or form comedic, and that it's just a fucking song designed to make the audience feel good and forget the drivel that came before it. It's a song that has no jokes in it, and is designed purely to get the audience chanting and finish on a high despite it lacking anything that resembles stand up comedy.

I'll scream in his face as he maintains his professionalism and assures the room that it's good for men to talk about their feelings as we don't do it enough and this is why men commit suicide ins such large numbers. Then I'll take out the knife I've snuck into the room and everyone will gasp.

I'll look John Ryan dead in the eyes and correct him. "No, John" I'll say "I'm killing myself because of you." At which point I will draw the sharpened blade across my jugular, spraying his smug, pudgy face with my blood as he instinctively blinks to protect his vision. Gary the first aider will faint because he's a fucking faggot and only went on the course to get the day off, while the rest will vomit. John Ryan will turn to run, but will slip on the vomit, falling backwards and fracturing his skull, as his blood mixes with mine, I fall to my knees whilst everything goes black. My dying wish will be that John Ryan survives, but is paralysed from the neck down and mute because of the trauma.

Chapter 8: Racial slurs: when to use them

This will be a handy guide that you can cut out and keep and refer to when you're unsure of how to proceed.

When to use a racial slur: when you're sure there aren't any in.

When not to use a racial slur: when there's at least one in.

PRO TIP: how come *they* can say the 'N' Word but *we* can't?

Chapter 9: Introducing a woman: how to lower expectations

In these times of diversity, it is likely that you will have to bring a comedienne on to the stage to entertain the punters. When this happens, it is important that you set the tone so that when the woman comes on she feels comfortable in her own skin and isn't worried about any preconceived sexist assumptions that the audience might have.

Physical touch is a great way to reassure an aspiring comedienne, so get them used to this by gently stroking their arm whenever you speak to them. When introducing them on stage, a firm handshake and a gentle pat on the bum are great confidence boosters that show the audience you consider this woman an equal.

Obviously, the gig is about to take a turn for the worse, so you need to make sure you've saved your A material for when she's got off and you need to get the gig back on track. Always make reference to the fact that the woman has performed some sort of sexual favour on you, as this is highly original and is very rarely done.

The key thing is to warn the audience about what is about to happen. This goes for whenever you introduce any kind of novelty act, as it's not fair on both the performer or audience if they aren't properly prepared. You want the comedienne to have as big a chance as possible of almost doing well.

The problem is that lots of women have many different experiences and opinions on life, and these are very rarely heard in comedy clubs. Mercifully, it is men who control this medium and as such, it is a highly male environment with many conceptions and assumptions formed around the male point of view. This is why comedy works. When a woman comes on stage, this gets all fucked up.

PRO TIP: women have menstrual cycles and can be irrational which is probably why they aren't responding to your green room flirting

Comediennes (or woman comedians) tend to talk from their perspective, rather than the perspective that we all know and love. Granted, there are many women in the audience and I'm sure they too can understand comedy at a very basic level. But women hate women, and as such a woman on stage represents a direct threat to the women in the audience and the comedienne will be quickly scowled at. It is up to you as the compere to deal with this dynamic.

A good way to introduce a woman is to announce that "we're about to get a woman on stage now" and leave a long, dramatic pause. Let the information sink in before telling them that you are not joking. The next minute is very important, as you have to keep the laughs rolling as people begin to walk out. You can usually stop some of the audience leaving by reassuring them that the woman is only doing an open spot and that the comedy will resume very soon.

What is VERY IMPORTANT is that you do all of this out of the ear shot of the comedienne. Women can be very sensitive, and we must allow them to try their best before failing. Women have a right, just like you, to get on stage and tell jokes. Just because you don't agree with it doesn't mean you have to bring your politics to the stage.

On the circuit, we all muck in together and it is up to us to change attitudes and move forward. It's 2018 for goodness sake, and here you are worried about making a living when this poor woman is having to endure a chorus of boos and things being thrown at her. If that's the world you want, go and live in Saudi Arabia.

Victoria Wood was a woman, and she was funny.

Chapter 10: But what if I'm a woman: when nature hates you

Being a woman compere is no easy task. Indeed, I'm perhaps not even qualified to speak on such an issue. I'm not a woman, and have never had to endure the creeping, horrible sexism that most female comedians have had to endure. The horrible feeling of people sinking into their chairs when you're introduced, and having to deal with the non-sensical prejudice of an audience so used to men wandering on stage in an overly confident manner, that you question your own reasons for doing stand up comedy.

Men can be distinctly average and not even good looking, but we're so conditioned to laughing at men and their wacky exploits that we give them a pass. Women are given a higher bar to leap, and the slightest deviation can result in ever more ridiculous theories about whether or not women can be funny.

I have no doubt that women can be incredibly funny, but can they be good comperes? Do they have the necessary ability to think on their feet and be in the moment? Do they have the improvisational skills required to create spontaneous laughter, and can they do it at a higher standard than the shitty standard we seem to let men get away with?

My answer is: no. Our social conditioning is so strong that any women in a role of authority will immediately trigger Oedipal thoughts in the audience. The idea of gouging ones eyes out is never pleasurable and not one that is conducive to comedy. I myself have always been sexually attracted to my mother, and as such I avoid female authority figures for fear that one day I might end up balls deep in my Mum's arse, enjoying her soothing reassurance that I am indeed a very good boy.

But, if you are a woman reading this, I will do my best here to try and give you a fighting chance.

PRO TIP: you've had a shit gig if someone doesn't come up to you afterwards and tell you that they don't normally find women funny

Get the audience onside early by reassuring them that you do part time cleaning on the side to help supplement your income as a stand up comedian. This will help the audience to be reassured that you understand your gender role and it's place in society, and that you pose no threat to anyone in the audience. Maybe take a duster on stage with you to help emphasise this, or at least keep your uniform on from when you've been at work that day.

You will not be able to command the audience's respect, but you will be able to command their sympathy. The first 30 seconds when on stage are incredibly important, so make sure that you wince in pain and hold your stomach within that first half a minute. You have to be convincing about this, and then not want to talk about it if anyone asks what the problem is. The audience will assume that you are having some period pains, and will give you sympathy for soldiering on, rather than judging you for not being a man.

Do NOT talk about sex. This is not in the domain of women, and ESPECIALLY do not talk about fanny farts. Fanny farts are not funny in any way shape or form - they are disgusting and to be avoided at any cost. In fact, if you are reading this now and think that the trapping of air inside a woman's dick hole being expelled audibly and forcefully is humorous, then you need to go and have good look at yourself in the mirror. Further, repeated fanny farts caused by vigorous thrusting of a penis and/or dildo is not a cause for laughing and not a topic for humour. If you reference a fanny fart whilst compering, and the resemblance it has in it's sound to a plunger being used on a particularly stubborn sink blockage, then you should hand in your mic at the door and get rid of any idea of what it is you think comedy is.

Remember: women are 50% of the population but only 24% of the funny population. Don't aim too high, and remember that sometimes it better to not try. Yes, sexism is awful, but sometimes it's also correct. Comedy is always in need of ineffective show managers, so all hope is not lost.

Chapter 11: Calling an interval: do it like a boss

You've smashed the opening. The roof has been removed and the first act has been unable to follow you. You've followed all of my guidance and now you walk back on stage to give the audience permission to go and excrete bodily waste in the appropriate areas (your Mum's mouth for example).

You walk on stage and shake hands with the departing act - but you're frozen. You have no idea what to do. You stand there as the audience stares at you, waiting to be told what to do like the obedient little sluts that they are. You're now naked, and your high school maths teacher is wanking directly into your face.

You wake up, sweat pouring from your face as you realise that you are not prepared for the most important part of being a compere: calling an interval.

Ever since Bill Hicks tore up the rule back way back in the early 90s, comedians have had no idea how to call an interval. Most comperes wander up on stage and continually hit themselves in the face until the audience becomes so uncomfortable that they just get up and go to the bar. A small number of comics will openly soil themselves and allow the smell to take care of proceedings. Don't be this guy. Be the guy you've always wanted to be. Call that interval like another fucking boss.

The key thing is that this is YOUR time on stage, and you deserve respect. The audience are to stay in their seats until you've given them permission to leave. Walk on and tell them that you have an announcement to make before they leave. Say it with confidence, into the microphone, and leave a dramatic pause. Lick you lips, then whisper gently into the microphone the way you would whisper into a child's ear to tell them it was "our little secret" and say:

'Ladies and gentlemen, it is time for your interval. Gender is a social construct. Take your glasses back to the bar, please buy a raffle ticket.'

People think calling an interval is easy and perfunctory, and as such it is criminally overlooked by most books on compering, in particular Freddy Quinne's travesty of a book. You are the audience's guide. Their confidant. You can't abuse that power or their trust. You must use it for the greater good and the interval is where it matters most.

PRO TIP: fist bump all black acts: never shake their hand

Chapter 12: Chatting to the audience during an interval: getting that dick wet

So far, you've used your power for good. You've got the audience onside, earned their trust, and you've changed their view on society by calling the interval in a socially responsible fashion. Now, it's time to abuse that power and take advantage of the low level of celebrity you've managed to build for yourself over the previous 15 minutes or so. You've used high quality banter and repeated references to the The Tube if you're one of those London cunts who thinks everything that comes out their mouths is dynamite. You cunts can fuck right off with your bringer gigs and your bullshit alternative scene that just caters to sex pests and rapists. Many good things came out of the #metoo movement but one of the best was exposing those hypocritical fuckers who championed a woman's right to work without harassment on the one hand, whilst trying to finger fuck them with other. Die you sneaky fucking pieces of shit. Die in front of your mothers.

Getting your dick wet need not be an arduous task, but it's certainly fraught with danger, as you still have the rest of the show to compere. My advice would be to always go for a married woman, preferably one that is married to the promoter and is obviously sex starved. Lots of compering books won't mention this topic ***coughs*** *Freddy's book* ***coughs*** but you need to be prepared.

Yes, you might be happily married, but it isn't going to last, and in today's more permissive society, a polyamorous lifestyle isn't just preferable, it is inevitable. More and more men are born with micro penises, and more of them are taking to the stage in a bid to compensate for their pathetic manhood, so it makes sense to not only learn to charm an audience for the good of comedy, it also makes sense to charm a woman into the disabled toilets for a fast fuck.

PRO TIP: covering her mouth helps to prevent you being caught and helps to stop her removing consent

Chatting up a member of the audience is a lot like chatting to the audience as a whole. Start off with a greeting, and then move on to asking for her name and occupation. When she tells you what she does for a living, try and shoe horn in a joke about what her favourite type of thing is that is to do specifically with that job. This is a tried and tested method for compering, and it works just as well when you're trying to secure a tit fuck cum fest.
Some examples:

Occupation	What's your favourite type of…
Nurse	Illness
Accountant	Spreadsheet
Cleaner	Mop
Recruitment	Job
Radioligist	Bone
Electrician	Fuse
History teacher	Year
Maths teacher	Equation
Science teacher	Test Tube
Police officer	Crime
Web cam sex performer	Disgusting pervert

As you can see, this not at all hackneyed method of interacting is tailor made for getting some pussy.

"But what do I do when I've got day puss puss? How can I please her?"

This is not a question that a real compere would ask. A real compere would already be back in the green room telling the other lads what he's just been up to. Respect for women and women's pleasure is something that open spots do. You ain't no open spot no more, you're the real deal. Ain't nobody getting their dick wet at charity dos or open mic nights. Hell no! The is club level comedy. The pinnacle. This is money towards accommodation and a free drink/meal of your choosing up to the value of £10. You've made it! You're not bringing on fresh faced hopefuls looking for validation. Hell no! You're bringing on dead-behind-the-eyes comedians bemoaning the state of the circuit whilst doing nothing productive to change their own circumstances. You're not introducing new comedians trying out different material at every gig. Hell no! You're introducing men who complain that too many women are on telly now and why can't your tried and tested set of 20 years get a fucking chance on Netflix?

You're a compere now. You're getting that dick wet and that's all that matters. The other acts are doubling because they can actually do sets.

Chapter 13: Closing the show: "I'm on Twitter…"

The night couldn't have gone any better. You've changed the game, son!

But what if they forget you?

As the audience files out, be sure to remind them where they can get hold of you if they need anything else. The more desperate you sound the better, but try and make it sound like you don't really care if they follow you on any of the social media platforms. Lots of acts consider a social media platform to be a waste of time. They couldn't be more wrong. The more followers you have, the more other comedians will respect you. It's all about an online presence now.

The key thing here is to be unoriginal. Whatever you see a contemporary do, copy it as soon as possible. Remember, on Facebook a video only has to be viewed for 3 seconds for it to count as a view, so make sure you have a good title. Something like "Comedian copies another comedian" or "Another comedy club plays catch up" will work a treat.

One thing I've started doing is offering personal training to audience members who are great big fat fucks. I offer diet plans and one to one training sessions, working on the basic barbell lifts of the Squat, Bench Press, Deadlift and Press.

PRO TIP: kill all the momentum of the gig by listing every social media platform you're on you fucking despicable cunt

We start with a linear progression over three to four months, building a good base of strength before moving on to more complex programming. Proficiency of technique is vital, so correct form when performing the lifts is not only necessary to prevent injury, but to exercise the most amount of muscles mass over the most effective range of motion.

I start off with teaching the squat, working up to a good set of 5 as your starting weight. During your next session, you will add 5kg to that weight and perform squats at your working weight for 3 sets of 5. At your next session, we will again increase the weight, possibly by 5kg or maybe just 2.5kg. Regardless, once we switch to 2.5kg jumps per session, we stick to that and make sure you are eating and sleeping enough to recover.

At this early stage, you shouldn't worry too much about what you look like and just be focusing on lifting more and more weight until we've got your squat up to a good standard.

Also after a gig, why not sell some of your merchandise? You probably think this is stupid, but these idiots are more than likely pissed and will probably buy a CD they'll never listen to if it's only a fiver.

Colin Cole used to sell T-Shirts ffs. AND PEOPLE BOUGHT THEM.

Any shame you feel will be removed when you get that cold hard cash in your hands. No receipts either, so that fucker won't be recorded and HMRC can suck on your fingers and look all sexy while you wank yourself silly.

You might get asked for selfies after gigs, and although this can be embarrassing, it's a great way to cop a feel of some sexy ladies. Don't be subtle either, as you can pass off most things as a joke and they'll totally be into it. Hand on the waist, then slide it down past their arse and give one of the cheeks a little squeeze. She'll love it mate!

Once you are back in your car, avoid looking at yourself in the rear view mirror. What have you become? When you started this you were so full of hope. Dreams. You wanted to make the whole world laugh and your wife was with you for the journey. Now she can't even stand the sight of you and she's gaining a hell of a lot of weight. The car is so lonely, you don't bother with your seat belt as you drive away, audience members recognise you as you wave and smile from a car that you can't afford. £50 on a Thursday with a two hour drive to look forward to. The M6 is shut, and God hates you that little bit more than he did earlier.

70mph. 80mph. 90mph. What would happen now if I just swerved into a barrier? The beeping of the seat belt warning is rhythmic, as the crushing silence of solitude begs you to drive into the abyss, the laughs and applause but distant memories of those moments when you felt alive. Your life insurance will pay out, but why should that bitch get anything?

Blue lights flash behind but they are not for you, as the police car overtakes you to a more deserving human. Your weekend is free as you push the car to 100mph, with next weekend completely empty. The phone rings: it's The Comedy Store. Tears in your eyes, you answer. Your open spot went well, but they'd like to see you again in a year. Would you like to book a spot in now?

What they find of you is a mess, but if you'd survived, you'd only have gotten 5 minutes out of it, not an entire show like a proper comic

FURTHER READING

The Protocols of the Elders of Zion

Children of The Matrix - David Icke

Dangerous - Milo Yiannopoulos

AIDS: is it real? - Cardinal O'Reilly

Solving 9-11: The Deception That Changed the World - Christopher Bollyn

Day Bang: How to casually pick up women - Roosh V

Manufacturing Consent - Noam Chomsky

Mountain Climbing - Hugo First

How to keep a clean scalp - Dan Druff

Amphibians - Newt and Sally Mander

How to ass fuck - Ben Dover and Phil Mcavity

Fulfilling your man with tit wanks - E. Norma Stits

Quinn(e)tesential Guide to Compering - Freddy Quinne

INDEX

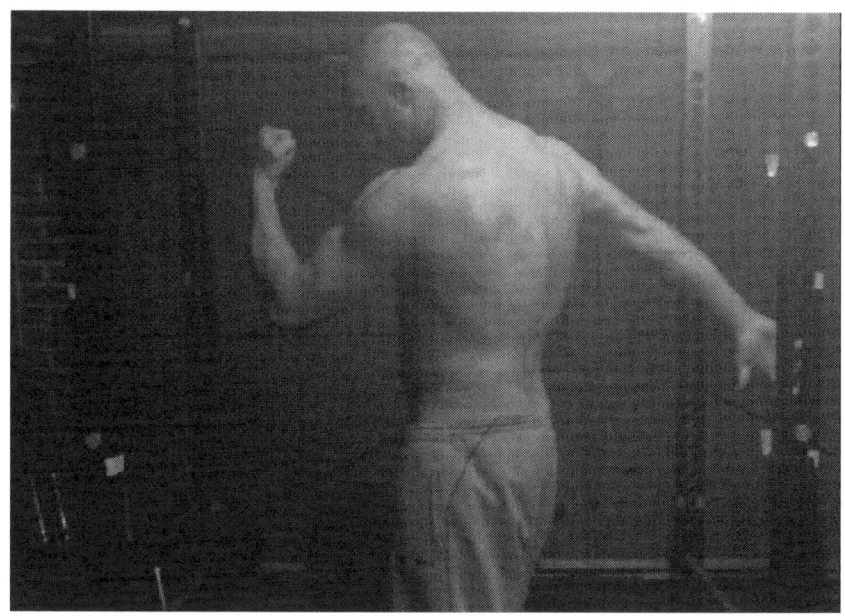

Dave Longley is a stand up comedian. Maybe listen to his podcast on iTunes? It's called ARGUING FOR THE SAKE OF ARGUING.

Dave is also on twitter. And Facebook.

Who the fuck isn't?

Printed in Great Britain
by Amazon